AKAVAK

AKAVAK
An Eskimo Journey

Written and illustrated by
James Houston

Longmans Canada Limited

Longmans Canada Limited
55 Barber Greene Road
Don Mills, Ontario

Printed in the United States of America

ᐃᓄᖃᑏᖑ ᑭᑭᑕᔾᒥᐅᑖᖑᖏ: ᐊᒍᐊᓯᑎᖓᒡ
ᓴᕙᒍᐊᑕᖓᓂᐦ. ᐃᕐᐸᒍᐊᓂᑕ.
ᐅᓂᐸᐅᖅᐸᐅᓴᓂᐅ.
ᓴᐅᒥᖅ

To the people of Baffin Island:
sea hunters, carvers, singers,
possessors of great stories.

The left handed.

AKAVAK

AKAVAK awoke slowly, feeling the soft warmth of the caribou-skin robes against his naked body.

He listened but could not hear the wind giants that had tried to bury the snowhouse for days. Yes, they were gone now. Everything was deadly silent.

He lay in the midst of all his family on their wide skin-covered bed of snow in the igloo of his father. The big seal-oil lamp that gave light and heat to their house was almost out.

Akavak watched his breath rise slowly like steam toward the domed ceiling, then freeze into small white crystals and fall onto the dark furs that spread across the bed.

In the darkness, Akavak heard his grandfather sit up, unroll the parka he had used for a pillow, and draw it slowly over his head. He heard him lean forward, puffing heavily as he pulled on his dogskin pants and his knee-high sealskin boots. Then the old man slid out from between the warm furs and heaved himself down off the wide sleeping platform. Bending low, he made his way along the narrow snow passage that twisted through the meat porch and upward to the entrance.

When his grandfather stepped outside of the snowhouse, he coughed harshly as he breathed in the sharp, searing cold of the morning air. Then Akavak heard him whistle three times and knew he must be calling to the night spirits that fling their weird, glowing patterns among the stars. This whistling surely meant that he could see the northern lights and that at last the wind giants had swept the whole sky clear.

As the old man moved away from the entrance of the igloo, Akavak heard the snow squealing in pain beneath his feet. It must be very cold.

Akavak looked toward his father, now awake, supporting his weight on one elbow. His dark eyes sparkled, and his strong white teeth flashed in the half dark as they reflected the flickering light of the stone lamp.

"Your grandfather must see his brother before he dies," said Akavak's father. "Long ago he promised to do this. Now he grows old, and there is only a little time. You are the one who must help him.

"His brother's land we call the Kokjuak. It lies to the north. There a mighty river flows into the sea. I have never seen that place, but it is said that great herds of walrus come to the very edge of the ice. In summer countless birds lay their eggs on the cliffs. When the moon is full in spring and again in autumn, the whole river is alive with fish.

"The way to that good land is long and hard. You must avoid the high mountains that stretch inland. Stay on the coast and travel on the sea ice. There are no people to help you on the way, for the huge tidal flats prevent hunting there during the time of

10

open water. It is a starving place between our last cache of food and the Kokjuak. There is a big fjord you must cross. Sometimes thin ice makes that impossible. If that is so, perhaps you should return here.

"I cannot take your grandfather there," Akavak's father added, "because we have not enough meat in our caches. In order to feed this family, I must hunt every day that the weather allows. So, this long journey falls to you. Go with him as he has asked and care for him, for his legs have grown stiff and often his eyes water in the wind until he cannot see. Sometimes when the day ends, you will see him tremble with the cold. But he will not complain. Then you must stop early and help him build a snowhouse.

"Remember that he is strong and determined and almost always wise. He knows the way to the land of his brother, for he traveled that way long ago when he was a young man. Listen to the words he says to you and learn from him, for that is the way in which all knowledge has come to this family. No man can build a better snowhouse, and when he commands that team of dogs, it will move for him as though it were his legs and arms, a part of himself.

"But sometimes now he does not hear the words that are spoken to him, and his eyes stare, and his spirit seems to go away from him and wander to some distant place, for he is very old. If he does not seem to hear you and his spirit appears to leave him, you must then be careful and decide everything for him.

"Take care of him and of yourself. Go with health and strength. That is what I have to say to you."

"Yes," answered Akavak, for it was the only word he could find to say to his father.

Akavak sat up quickly and drew on his warm fur parka and pants. This immense journey would take him into a new world, and he was secretly delighted. Until now he had never traveled more than two sleeps away from this place where he had been born fewer than fourteen winters before. Also, he had rarely seen a stranger.

Samatak, his mother, was a wise and kindly woman. Silently she reached up to the drying rack beside her place on the bed and handed him warm caribou-skin stockings and new sealskin boots that she had finished making in the night.

With nervous wonder in her voice, she whispered to Akavak, "Last night while you were sleeping, your grandfather told us many things about his youth when he lived in the far-off land of

his brother. I understand now why he wishes to return to that place. He gave us names to be used for children in this family that have not yet been born, for he was anxious to have me understand their importance. I believe that he does not expect to return here. What will become of you? I think of you both: one too young and one too old for such a journey. I am filled with fear."

She watched her son's handsome smooth-skinned face, his long blue-black hair, and the quick movements of his strong arms. She tried desperately to engrave his image on her mind forever, for she might never see her son alive again.

Akavak made his way out of the snowhouse and stood upright at the end of the entrance passage, feeling his nostrils pinch together in the burning cold. The trail would be hard and wind-swept, excellent for traveling. Around the four igloos of the camp, the snow stretched away white, then turned blue-gray, and finally disappeared in the night shadows that seemed to rise upward and blend with the star-filled sky.

Some of the sled dogs that had slept beneath the snow during the blizzard were sitting up now, still stiff with sleep. Their thick tails were curled tightly across their feet, and their backs were humped against the crackling cold. Akavak's grandfather had pulled down all the hunting gear and the coiled dog lines from their places on top of the snowhouse. He had his sealskin hunting bag slung across his shoulders. It contained all the things he needed to survive. His raised hood almost covered his long gray hair and the wide cheekbones of his wrinkled face. He was ready to travel.

Akavak's father followed him out of the igloo. Standing

together, they watched the old man walking stiff-legged but fast across the hard-packed drifts. He headed toward the high meat cache. With the meat hook, he reached up and caught the skin bag of frozen walrus meat and jerked it down.

"He is leaving this morning—that much is sure," said Akavak's father. "Help him to load the meat on the sled and lash it tightly. It is enough to last you until you reach our cache at the big fjord. The dogs will run well with empty stomachs. Feed them when you camp tonight."

As dawn turned the sky gray-green in the east, Akavak heard the sea ice crack and moan as it was forced upward by the morning tide. A faint wind rose with the day, causing the fine snow to drift like smoke across the land. The wind ran its icy fingers beneath the warmth of Akavak's fur parka until he shuddered with the cold and was anxious to go, to be free, to run beside the dogs and make his body warm again.

When the sled was loaded and the dogs were hitched to their long lines, the old man stood before each person, looking straight into their eyes. Two of the neighboring women with babies on their backs opened their hoods so that the children might see him, perhaps for the last time.

"*Tugvaosialunasik.* Farewell to all of you," he called out in a strong voice.

He then turned away from the people of the four snowhouses who had gathered to see him depart. He started off alone on foot, using the chisel end of his slender seal harpoon to feel his way. Skillfully he chose the best path for the dog team among the jagged teeth of barrier ice that had been thrown up by the great

15

tides. When he reached the smooth ice of the sea itself, he turned swiftly northward, holding himself upright, trying to look like a much younger man, for he knew that every eye in the village was upon him and he wished to leave them with a feeling of hope.

Akavak returned to the sled, after seeing that the six dogs were properly harnessed, and stood before the small group of men, women, and children. They were his family: his uncles, aunts, and cousins. The women hopped from one foot to the other trying to drive out the cold. They hummed soft songs and drew their fur hoods tight to keep the naked babies they carried from crying.

Akavak's father said, "At this time of the year, your grandfather's brother should be camped at the mouth of the giant river. Remain on the sea ice and follow the coast. That way you should not get lost. Beware of the mountains, son of mine." He paused, and then he said again, "Keep away from the mountains."

Then his father dealt Akavak a powerful blow on the side of the head, a thing he had never done before, for such a show of affection was never made to sons but was used only between full-grown men who were hunting companions or the best of friends. His father turned away, perhaps because he had shown his love so clearly, and walked quickly toward the igloos.

Akavak's mother and sister stood beside him, stock still, so gripped by fear that they could not feel the cold. His sister reached into her hood and drew out a new pair of fur mitts that she tucked under the lashings of the sled.

Akavak looked at her and smiled, remembering the good times they had had together. Then, without a word, he turned away, as was the custom of young men. Akavak drove his weight against

16

the sled, and as it started to move, he called out to the dogs that whined and howled, eager for the trail, and they dashed forward. His sister and all the older children leaped onto the moving sled. The dogs followed the old man's path down through the sharp hummocks of the shore ice and out onto the hard flat snow that covered the frozen sea. Akavak's cousins laughed with delight at the speeding sled, as one by one they tumbled off, shouting, calling farewell to him.

His sister did not laugh. She was the last to leave the sled.

Akavak looked back and saw her standing alone in the flat whiteness, growing smaller as the distance increased. He raised his hand to her. So full of loneliness was she that she could not wave to him, and, turning, she walked slowly back to the village, her hands covering her face.

The team pulled together, running fast, quickly overtaking the old man. He watched them as they passed him—first the lead dog, a lean clever female named Nowyah. She would obey the driver

quickly, going to the right or left at his command. Next came the big dog Pasti. Strong as a bear he was, black, with wide shoulders and a deep chest for pulling heavy loads. Then came Kojo, the fighter, gray and lean, with the long legs and the wicked eyes of a wolf. Following them, each hitched to the sled on a separate line, came the other three dogs, young, strong, and always hungry, still learning to pull within the team.

When the sled itself reached the old man, he ran to it and jumped on. He sat beside Akavak and placed his legs straight out before him. He pushed back his hood to cool himself and looked around.

Akavak watched him shading his old eyes from the light. At first he searched the flat level of the frozen sea and then looked inland, scanning the jagged white mountains that rose along the coast.

"Go there," said his grandfather, pointing to a place far before them where the mountains plunged into the sea and rose again as a rock-bound island. "We will pass through those narrows, and just beyond we will build our snowhouse for the night. Mark it well, for it will be dark by the time we reach that place."

At noon they stopped the sled and untangled the long dog lines. When they were ready to start again, Akavak drew one of the caribou sleeping skins across his grandfather's legs. The old man looked proudly away toward the narrows and did not seem to notice, but he did not remove the warm skin.

Akavak sometimes ran and sometimes rested on the sled, often calling encouragement to the dogs, guiding the course of the sled so that it was always pointed in the right direction.

It was fully night when they passed through the narrows and headed for the long, sloping shore. The moon was almost full and rode brightly among the stars. The snow sparkled all around them in its light.

The old man took up a bone wand, thin as an arrow and twice as long. With this he walked some distance, carefully probing into the hard, deep drifts. He seemed to be listening as he drove the point gently downward, feeling the texture of the snow. He walked further and probed again. Then he walked in a circle. Finally satisfied, he straightened up and called to Akavak, "Bring the snow knife."

With the long ivory knife, Akavak's grandfather first removed a large wedge of snow. Then he cut a big block, lifted it, and set it on the surface. He cut more blocks, placing them in a ring around himself. Then he started a second row spiraling upward.

Akavak chinked the outside of the blocks with fine snow, filling every crack. Although his grandfather worked slowly in the biting cold, he cut the blocks with great skill, and each one fitted perfectly. He remained within the ring, building from inside, slowly walling himself out of Akavak's sight.

When the dome was completed, the old man cut a neat entrance in the base of the snow wall, and Akavak heard him beating the snow out of his clothing with the knife. Akavak pushed the stone traveling lamp and sleeping skins inside. Then he fed the dogs, watching them devour the chunks of frozen walrus meat. Satisfied, they curled on the new snow, their tails placed protectively over their noses.

When he crawled inside the igloo, dragging the bag of meat after him, Akavak found his grandfather holding a bow drill in his mouth, whirling it with his hands until the shavings in the wood socket smoked and burned. He lighted the wick in the seal-oil lamp, and the new snowhouse glowed in the reflected light. Akavak beat the snow out of his own clothing and the sleeping skins and unwrapped a packet containing choice pieces of seal meat. The meat was frozen hard, but when they sliced it thinly, it seemed to melt in their mouths. Akavak and his grandfather ate a good deal of it and drank quantities of ice water, for they were hungry, and, as was the custom, this was their only meal of the day.

When it was done, they lay back, side by side, wrapped in the warm furs. Just before he went to sleep, Akavak heard his grandfather laugh and say aloud, "I remember an old story about a tiny ground spider that one summer day crawled onto a boy's arm, and the boy drew back his hand to strike it. But the spider said to him in a thin voice, 'Don't kill me, or my grandchildren will be sad.' And the boy let him go, saying, 'Imagine, so small, and yet a grandfather.' "

They both laughed, and then Akavak's grandfather said, "A man grows old looking at the same hill behind his house. It feels good to travel once again."

They left the igloo at the first light of dawn, harnessed the dogs, and were traveling almost before Akavak was fully awake.

Six snowhouses they built and six nights they slept as they traveled northward along the frozen sea. Akavak wondered at the great mountains he saw for the first time and at the huge curling tongues of the glacier that reached down to the white sea. Each day was bitter cold, but they were glad, for the trail remained hard and the dogs ran swiftly, dragging the light sled with ease. They fed them well each night, for they knew that the cache that Akavak's father had made at the big fjord was full of rich walrus meat.

On the seventh day, they pressed forward at the old man's insistence until long after the moon had risen, and when they came to the edge of the big fjord, they could see the high stone cairn that marked the precious meat cache on the shore. By the light of the full moon, they also saw the tracks of a huge bear leading straight to it. Then, with horror, they discovered that the starving bear had ripped apart the rocks Akavak's father had so carefully set and frozen into place over the meat. The bear had devoured everything.

"It can't be helped," the old man said when he had examined the tracks. "The bear has gone far out on the sea ice many days ago. Already its paw marks are half filled with drifting snow. We could never find that bear. We will sleep here tonight, and in the

morning we will make our plan. We have lost food that would have allowed us to travel for half a moon, and we are left with nothing."

That night the dogs could only lick the stones of the empty meat cache and growl with anger at the smell of the bear.

When they crawled out of the snowhouse at dawn, the old man pointed across the misty flatness that stretched before them.

"That is the big fjord called Kingalik," he said. "It is a dangerous place at this time of the year. The strong tides force their way into the fjord and wear the ice thin, but with the hard snow covering, you cannot see many of the holes. Men have died here, and whole dog teams have been lost through the ice. We must cross it if we wish to reach my brother's land. Come now, I will show you the way."

They drove the team off the land and out onto the sea ice. Great clouds of white fog rose into the air. Akavak's grandfather waved his arm and called to Nowyah, heading the sled between the rolling banks of fog. Although they could not see any openings in the ice, they knew the holes were there since the fog was caused by open sea water striking the deadly cold of the Arctic air.

The old man called to the team, and the dogs halted instantly. He rose from the sled, and taking the harpoon, he moved quickly forward, then stopped. Cautiously using the sharp bone chisel on the end of the harpoon, he jabbed through the thin snow surface to the ice below. Feeling that it was safe, he walked forward, and the dogs followed.

Before his grandfather had gone a dozen steps, Akavak saw the bone chisel break through the ice. Dark water flooded over the snow at the old man's feet. Moving as lightly as a white fox, the old man circled the weak place in the ice, for if he placed his foot upon it, he would surely have plunged into the freezing water.

He had not gone many steps farther when his chisel broke the ice again, and he quickly changed his course. The dogs followed him, crouching, their legs spread, fully aware of the danger. Akavak guided the sled and wondered at the path his grandfather set for them, for although the snow looked the same to him, his grandfather seemed to sense the bad places.

As they moved slowly forward, a wind blew in from the sea, causing the freezing fog to drift across the whole fjord, and they could no longer tell where the open places lay. Still the old man stiffly made his way onward, prodding the snow covering, turning this way and that, trying to find a path through the treacherous holes in the thin ice.

Then Akavak saw his grandfather suddenly fall flat on his back, his arms and legs outstretched. The ice had broken before him. His feet were in the water, but by falling, he had managed to spread his weight upon the thin ice. Quick as a weasel, he wriggled backward, away from the gaping black hole. Then he got onto his hands and knees and crawled cautiously until he could rise to his feet and walk back to the sled.

"We can go no farther," he said in a sad and weary voice. "The ice is too thin, too dangerous, and the fog blowing in makes it worse every moment. See, even now it hides our tracks back to the land."

Suddenly in the mistiness before them, they heard a strange snorting and blowing and a violent thrashing of water. The sound came to them again and again.

"What is that?" whispered Akavak, for he greatly feared this deadly place.

"*Agalingwak!*" cried the old man. "Narwhal, great spotted beasts, four times the length of a man, with a long, thin ivory tusk thrusting out before them."

Straining their eyes, Akavak and his grandfather finally saw the narwhal through open patches in the heavy mists. Many of them were plunging upward, gasping for air at the breathing holes in the ice.

"Oh, how I long to drive my harpoon into one of those great beasts of the sea," cried his grandfather, his arms outspread with excitement. Yet he dared not move a step forward on this treacherous ice.

"There before you is all the meat we need for many winters, but we cannot have it. Tonight the whales will keep these holes open and leave when the tide changes. There is no help for it. We must go back."

They turned the team carefully. Akavak walked ahead, and the old man rode on the sled. They searched desperately for their earlier trail. As the fog thickened, Akavak had sometimes to feel in the snow for the old sled tracks, finding them in the darkness with his bare hands.

When at last they arrived back at the snowhouse they had left that morning, they went to bed tired, hungry, and full of despair.

When Akavak awoke, he saw that his grandfather had already left the igloo. Akavak dressed quickly and crawled outside. In the faint light of morning, his grandfather walked toward him holding four ptarmigan. Small white feathered birds they were, with furry feet and dark rich flesh. Carefully the old man threw one to Nowyah and one to Pasti. Each dog caught the bird in its mouth and gulped it down, bones, feathers, and all, before the rest of the team could fight for it.

Inside the snowhouse, Akavak and his grandfather squatted on their heels and pulled the warm birds apart, devouring every scrap of blood and meat, sucking each bone clean. Finally they lined the insides of their boot bottoms with the softest feathers.

"We will travel up the big fjord," said the old man, "and see if we can find some other place to cross."

This they did, trying many times throughout that day and the following day to find a way over the treacherous ice. But they were always driven back.

On the third morning, they could see the end of the big fjord and a valley where a narrow frozen torrent twisted down from the mountains to the sea. As the sun rose, it lighted the steep red granite cliffs that stood on the opposite side of the fjord and revealed the rough tumble of ice that stretched beyond their view along the base of the cliffs.

"Even if we could cross the fjord at this place," said the old man, "we could not hope to climb those cliffs or travel through that rough ice along the opposite shore.

28

"There are only two things we can do. We can return home, or we can travel up that river valley you see before you and cross the high glacier into the mountains. Whatever we do, we must move quickly, for we have no food. Traveling to my brother's land from here is shorter than to return home."

"My father said that we should keep out of the mountains," answered Akavak boldly. "He said that we should beware of the mountains."

"Yes, yes," said his grandfather impatiently, "but your father does not know the mountains as I do. I traveled across this glacier before he was born. I know the way across the high plateau that leads to my brother's camp. I shall show you that trail. I long to move in the mountains again. Once we reach the plateau, we need only slide down the other side, and we will arrive in my brother's land.

"It is hard traveling in the mountains, but it is wonderful to see. Up there among the clouds, you can feel your back against the sky. Even the snow geese in summer fly far below you. Grandson of mine, would you like to go that way? Would you like to see the high place?"

"I don't know," said Akavak slowly. And he added, "My father said we should stay near the sea."

His grandfather did not seem to hear him.

"The weather is fine now, and we cannot wait longer," said the old man. "I am eager to end this journey.

"Musk ox, great black beasts of the high plain, live in the mountains, and we shall have them to eat and to feed our dogs. It is the only way."

What could Akavak say to such a wise and powerful man, the one who had taught his father? He could say no more. He could only help him to reach the far camp of his brother, or he would surely seem to be a coward, one who at the first hint of danger rushes back to his own snowhouse to hide among the women.

Looking straight at his grandfather, Akavak opened his eyes wide to show agreement.

His grandfather stood up stiffly, calling to the dogs, urging them toward the frozen river. The weather was cold and clear, and the sun was held in a huge silver ring of light. The snow on the mountaintops caught the light and shimmered like white clouds seen in summer.

30

In the paleness of evening, they reached the very end of the big fjord and stopped at the twisted river. It was solid, glaring ice. They unharnessed the team and built a snowhouse on the edge of the land.

That night Akavak had a strange feeling as he shoved the sleeping skins into their new igloo, for he did not like the great icy wall of rock that rose behind him. He had heard endless tales of Igtuk, the boomer, a dreaded mountain spirit who runs in the high places, and of the Tornait, dwarf people who hide among the rocks. He was both excited and afraid, for the mountains seemed dangerously silent. His people were sea hunters, coastal people used to slim kayaks and the crushing ice of the sea but fearful of the high places and the terrible storms that raged there.

Akavak awoke once in the night and heard his grandfather call out in his sleep, shouting his brother's name again and again, and when he looked at the old man in the flickering light, he saw that his face was covered with sweat, although it was freezing cold in the snowhouse.

In the morning, with great care, they lashed their few possessions onto the sled and repaired the dog lines. Their path into the mountains would be a hard one.

From the first moment, their trail slanted upward. Akavak was never able to sit on the sled, and only at first could his grandfather ride. Akavak walked beside the sled, following along the river course, keeping the dogs away from the glare ice where they slipped and could not pull.

By noon, both Akavak and his grandfather were walking, and then pushing and shouting at the dogs, urging them forward. A big Arctic hare bounded away from them, but before Akavak could get the bow off the sled, a huge snowy owl swooped on silent wings over the team of dogs and, plunging downward, caught the hare. Still struggling, the feathered hunter and its prey disappeared from sight.

To his grandfather, Akavak said, "One has to be quick to stay alive in these mountains."

They camped that night at the bottom of a steep waterfall, frozen smooth and solid between two dark red walls of rock. The dogs moaned with weariness and with hunger.

"Is this the same path you took long ago?" Akavak asked his grandfather when they were wrapped in their sleeping skins.

"Yes, this is the river trail, and I remember these falls. It is a very difficult place."

In the first light of morning, Akavak's grandfather showed him some hand and foot holds in the ice and granite. Tying two long dog lines together, Akavak started the dangerous climb. Straight up the side of the frozen waterfall he went, until he was almost halfway. Then he slipped and fell back, arms outstretched. The dark rocks flashed past his eyes—then he landed in a deep bank of snow. All the wind was knocked out of him, and for some time he could not speak. As he started to test his arms and legs to see if they were broken, he saw his grandfather's worried face appear above him.

"Perhaps we should go back," said the old man, holding onto Akavak's arm. "Perhaps it is too hard. I cannot help you climb such a place."

As breath returned to Akavak, he remained on his back,

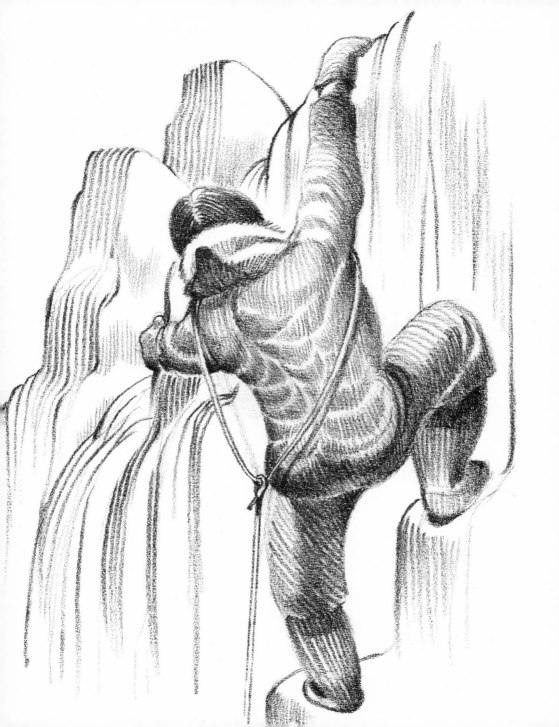

staring up at the frozen waterfall, his eyes searching for the jagged footholds.

"I will go up. I will climb that place," he said with determination, for now, like his grandfather, he could feel the magnetic power of the mountains, and he did not wish to turn back.

With the long dog line tied around his waist, he climbed again. He moved more carefully this time, testing every handhold, pressing his body close to the hard ice. When at last he reached the top and drew himself onto the flat ledge, he lay there, gasping for breath until his strength returned to him.

Then he stood up, and the old man called out to him, "Good! You have made it. Find a strong foothold, and I shall tie Nowyah so that you can pull her up to the ledge."

The old man pushed the lead dog up as far as he could, and then Akavak hauled her the rest of the way, hand over hand. She whined and struggled to find footholds, scrambling against the icy rock face. When she came over the edge and Akavak untied her, she licked his hand.

Akavak lowered the rope again. His grandfather tied on Kojo next, and Akavak attached the upper end of the line to Nowyah's harness. Together they hauled the big dog up the frozen falls. Working above and below, the grandfather tied each dog carefully, and Akavak and the team lifted each one to the ledge. Then the sled was stripped bare and raised, followed by the precious lamp wrapped in the sleeping robes.

It was almost dark when, with great care, Akavak, Nowyah, Pasti, and Kojo hauled the old man to the top.

For some time, Akavak and his grandfather squatted together

in the darkness, so tired they could not move. They themselves had worked like dogs all day and were starving, and yet their last snowhouse lay directly below them. Akavak threw down a chunk of snow onto its roof and laughed without joy, because it did not seem possible that it could be so close.

Slowly they went about building a new snowhouse. It was deadly cold in the mountains, and they feared a sudden storm. Akavak's back that had been wet with sweat turned clammy cold, and his bones trembled.

"We will reach the top tomorrow," said the old man. "If the weather stays clear, we will reach the top before dark."

In the flickering light of the lamp, Akavak drew off his damp parka and lay in the dry warmth of the sleeping skins. He seemed to see his grandfather for the first time. A strong, proud old man he was, his face brown and hard and seamed like the rocks of the mountains. His hair was almost white and hung to his shoulders. But his eyes were the most important part of him. They were half hidden under deep slanting lids that protected them from the wind and glaring snow, but when the black pupils of his eyes flashed, they were like two spots of sunlight on dark water. Akavak could tell by his grandfather's face that he had seen many things, good and bad. When his grandfather was young and in his full strength, he was famous as a drum dancer and singer. His hunting companions said that he had once harpooned and held a walrus until it ceased to live, and then with mighty strength he had pulled it out of the water onto the ice by himself. No man among their people had ever done this before. But now his strength was almost gone, and his big square hands with the wide powerful thumbs trembled when he tried to light the lamp.

When Akavak left the snowhouse in the morning, he saw long, thin white clouds flaring across the sky. These were driven by high winds far above them. His grandfather looked at them but said nothing. Akavak watched him hurrying to harness the tired, half-starving dogs.

They pushed forward once more, finding that the air was thin and hard to breathe. Akavak was so hungry that he sometimes lost all sense of time and seemed to float beside the sled.

He had been climbing in this trance for some while when he noticed that his grandfather was no longer beside the sled. Looking back down the trail, he saw him sitting hunched in the snow, his head on his knees.

Akavak halted the dogs and hurried back to help him.

"Go on. Go on," said the old man in a slow, thin voice. "I will rest here a while and then follow you to the top."

"No, Grandfather. You will come with me now. We must stay together," Akavak said with determination.

Akavak helped his grandfather up and supported him to the sled. Then he wrapped a caribou sleeping skin around his shoulders. The old man lay half on the sled but managed somehow to push with his feet, and in this way they started upward again. Akavak shouted at the dogs and beat on the wooden runners to frighten them, and they crept steadily forward.

Finally he could see the top, but he did not dare to rest in their slow passage upward, for the sky was darkening and clouds now hid the high peaks. The wind rushed in from the southwest, howling as it struck the frozen mountains.

Soon they were climbing the last rise, and then they suddenly stopped and stared. The wide glacier lay before them, gray and ancient, laced with new white snow. Beyond it stretched the great flat plain of the high plateau, in places blown entirely clear by the violent winds, so that huge patches of tundra and many stones shaped like skulls were exposed to sight.

The dogs lay down, and the travelers turned the sled onto its side, against the rising wind. They, too, lay down, waiting for their strength to return to them.

"Come," said the grandfather. "We must cross the glacier there at the narrow place. Beyond it we will build a snowhouse."

Slowly they followed the dogs, stumbling across the blinding whiteness of the glacier. Once they heard it creak and moan beneath their feet.

"I do not like this place," said Akavak's grandfather, and he slid the harpoon out from under the sled's lashings. He started to walk forward, feeling carefully before him with the bone chisel. But for once his keen instinct for danger warned him too late.

With an awesome "swoosh," the snow around Akavak collapsed and fell into a great yawning blue abyss. He watched with horror as the scrambling, howling dogs disappeared. Then, as though by evil magic, the sled beside him slipped away, and he could no longer see his grandfather. In the swirling snow, Akavak's foot caught on something as he started to plunge into the awful abyss. Half turning, flailing, gripping, he lost his mitts and felt his bare hands strike something solid. It was the edge of the ice wall. He held on for his life. The thunder below him died away, and everything was silent again.

His muscles ached with deadly weariness, and his bare hands grew numb against the ice. But still he waited, his eyes closed, holding on to life with his fingertips. How long before he, too, must fall?

He did not see the rough old hand reach over the edge of the abyss, but he felt it grasp him by the hood of his parka, and another hand took his wrist. A rasping voice called, "Kojo! Kojo!" and in another moment he felt a sealskin line lashed around his wrist.

The old man called, "Ush, ush," to the dog. Then Akavak felt his hood jerk upward, and his arm was nearly pulled from its socket as he was drawn up out of the gaping hole in the glacier.

The boy and the old man lay beside the open crevasse, too exhausted to move. Kojo, the starving dog that looked like a wolf, stood over them, with the dog line still attached to Akavak's wrist. For a moment it looked as though Kojo was the hunter and these creatures stretched on the snow were his prey.

Akavak's hands were white and would not bend. His grandfather held them under his own parka, against the warmth of his body until they burned like fire and the fingers could move once more. Then, because Akavak had no mitts, he drew his hands up into the long fur sleeves of his parka.

The sled and all the dogs were gone save Kojo. Akavak could scarcely believe the swiftness of death that had taken Nowjah, Pasti, and the others and buried them deep in the glacier forever.

The three staggered away from the awful blue hole and fearfully crossed the remaining tongue of the glacier. When they reached solid ground once more, they felt on their faces stinging grains of icy snow that blew down from the surrounding peaks. Slowly they made their way toward a small gully on the high plateau. It would give them some protection from the mighty force of the rising wind. They shambled on, the old man holding Kojo's broken harness for support. Akavak tried not to think of what they would do now. They had no food. Without dogs or sled, there could be no going back or forward from this frightening place.

Akavak saw it first, half buried in the snow. It was so old and frozen that the dog did not even smell it. Two great horns curved upward, and one empty eye socket stared at them from the whitened skull.

"*Umingmuk*," said his grandfather, "musk ox, long dead, killed by wolves perhaps."

"Nothing left," said Akavak sadly, kicking away the snow from the bare bones that lay scattered like gray driftwood among the useless tufts of long hair.

Bending over to examine it, the old man said, "That is a piece of skin, strong heavy skin," and he pried the end of a large stiff piece away from the frozen ground. Reaching into his hunting bag, he drew out a small knife and gave it to Akavak, together with one of his mitts.

"Cut away as large a piece as you can," he said. Then the old man stamped hard on the bleached skull, and the two big horns broke away.

"Bring these also," he said, and without another word he limped away toward the rocky cliff at the end of the little gully. In the wind, the caribou sleeping skin that was still wrapped around his hunched shoulders flapped like the wings of some ancient bird.

Akavak watched his grandfather as he edged along, carefully studying the cliff face, sometimes taking off his mitt to feel it. Then suddenly he dropped to his knees and started scraping and digging in a frenzied way. Akavak wondered if the time had come, as his father had warned, when his grandfather's spirit might wander away from him and he must take care of him.

With the knife, Akavak went on hacking and pulling at the useless frozen skin, looking at the gaping holes in it, knowing that it could have no warmth. With a jerk, he pulled free a large piece of the hide and straightened up.

He saw his grandfather walking slowly toward him. In his hands he held four stones. Wearily the old man choose a site and waved to Akavak to put the frozen hide down on the snow and place the stones on top. From his hunting bag, he drew a thin ivory blade and licked it until it was covered with a thin coating of ice and could be used to cut the heavy snow blocks. Together they worked and built a small strong igloo to stand against the forces of the mountain winds.

Once inside, Akavak's grandfather cleaned the snow out of a hollow in the largest stone and, taking a small pouch from his hunting bag, removed some frozen seal fat. He held a piece of this in his mouth to soften it. Next he cut a small piece off his inner clothing to serve as a wick, and then he whirled his bow drill in its wooden socket until the dry wood shavings smoldered and burned. Carefully he lit the oil-soaked wick, and it sputtered and burst into flame, casting a small warm glow inside the sparkling white of the new snow walls.

They placed the frozen musk-ox skin on the soft snow floor, and over this they spread the caribou skin the old man had worn around his shoulders. They lay down with Kojo between them, using the dog's body heat to keep them from freezing.

That night, the terrible wind screamed and thundered over

their small igloo, trying to tear it from the high plateau and fling it down the mountains. But their house was strong and round and carefully trimmed, with no corners for the wind to grasp, and as Akavak drew his head deep into his hood and hugged his arms next to his body inside his parka, he thought, "I am alive, and my grandfather is alive, and together we shall cross this high plateau and see the land of my great uncle that lies beyond these mountains." He said that to himself, again and again, until he drifted off to sleep. He dreamed of clever Nowyah, and Pasti the strong one, and the three young dogs lost to him forever.

When Akavak awoke, he heard the sharp click of stone against stone. He rolled over and saw his grandfather hunched beside the light, holding a flat stone in his hand. His grandfather judged the angle, then carefully struck the stone a sharp blow, causing a chip to fly off. Again and again he struck the flint, each time

examining the shape. Gradually, as the day wore on, the stone was formed into a sharp blade, almost as long as Akavak's hand.

On the following day, the wind continued to thunder against the house. Akavak and his grandfather chewed pieces of skin cut from their boot tops to ease their terrible hunger, but always the old man went on grinding and sharpening the chipped blade.

They slept again, and so dark and terrible was the storm around their house that they could not tell if it were night or day.

When they awoke, Akavak's grandfather said, "When I slept, I dreamed." As he spoke, he trimmed the dying lamp wick and squinted his old eyes into the flame. "I dreamed that I walked up along the shining path of the moon and flew among the stars. I could see all the mountains and the rivers and the sea beneath me. Great herds of caribou I saw, and mighty whales rolling in the sea, and huge flights of geese. Seeing these things seemed to ease my hunger. I was pleased to have such a night journey, but when I grew tired, I found that I did not have the power to return to the earth. I felt a great sadness, for I knew I would not see my son or my grandson again, or my brother who lives beyond this mountain, or his sons. My mind was full of grief that I had not visited them. That was all that I minded about leaving this earth.

"And when I awoke just now, I thought again and again that I am an old man and may never reach my brother's land, and my hand shall not touch his hand again."

Akavak could not answer his grandfather, but he knew that what he said was very important to him.

With the new stone blade, the old man showed his grandson how to shape and polish the musk-ox horns. Akavak then scraped out the hollow insides until they were smooth. When they were finished, he filled the new cups with snow scraped from the inside walls of the igloo and held them above the lamp until the snow melted and turned to water. As Akavak held the cups over the flame of the lamp, he thought that although the great storm held them like prisoners in the little house, he and his grandfather were always busy when they were awake, working to stay alive. They were determined to leave the mountain.

They slept and woke again with pangs of hunger, listening grimly to the raging storm.

The frozen musk-ox hide was now soft and soggy, having partly thawed from the heat of their bodies. Akavak held one end while his grandfather poured melted snow water from the musk-ox horns over the skin. When it was soaked, his grandfather twisted and rolled it tightly into a staff as tall as Akavak, and with thin strips cut from the hide, they bound the limp staff along its whole length. When this work was done, they were both weak and tired and went to sleep.

Akavak and the old man awoke in the lonely time just before dawn. The dog Kojo was snarling, drawing back his lips to show his big teeth. The hair on his neck bristled, and his yellow wolflike eyes glared at them wildly. Suddenly they both feared him, but although the old man held the stone blade ready, he did not want to kill the dog.

"Cut away the snow door," his grandfather said in a quiet voice.

Akavak quickly obeyed, and Kojo rushed out into the dying breath of the storm, howling in his madness.

"I think he will not go far," said the old man, "for he needs us as much as we need him in this strange place.

"Take this rolled musk-ox hide outside. Mind that it is straight, for I may need to use it as a staff to help me down off this mountain." As he spoke, he smiled weakly and handed Akavak his fur-lined mitts.

Outside, Akavak rolled the staff in the hard snow until it was straight and he could feel it start to freeze. Then he placed it on top of the snowhouse, safe from the teeth of the starving dog.

He stretched himself, glad to be free of the snowhouse after being held so many days a prisoner of the storm. The clouds were breaking open everywhere across the dark sky, and he could see the stars flashing their light down to him. The storm would pass before the true dawn came. This gave Akavak a feeling of hope and almost of joy, though he could not tell why, since they had no dogs, no sled, no food, and they must surely die on top of this lonely mountain.

Shivering with cold and hunger, he crawled back into the little snowhouse and went to sleep, dreaming of soft, delicious marrow from the cracked bones of caribou and the tender flesh of a young loon.

When he awoke, everything was deadly silent, for the wind had gone completely. His grandfather, who was always awake before Akavak, this time lay sound asleep, his face hidden. Only his breath rising in thin steam showed that he was alive. Akavak saw that all the seal oil was gone and the flame in the stone lamp was out. It was bitterly cold in the igloo.

Akavak cut away the door again and crawled out into the light of morning. A freezing fog had swept in around the mountains, and the peaks above him seemed to hover in the air like giant

ghosts. The snow around their house had been carved into weird shapes that flowed into one another. These wind-packed drifts were difficult to see because they cast no shadow in the foggy light.

After replacing the snow door, Akavak walked a little way up the gully. He was stiff and moved slowly. Through the eddying fog, he could see the great plain once again, now blown almost clear of snow. Rocks and gray tundra moss lay exposed from the violence of the wind. He wondered which direction he and his grandfather should follow.

Suddenly he saw them. They loomed out of the fog like footless

51

black monsters with huge humped shoulders. Their heads were down, and their black-tipped horns curved out sharply. At first, he counted as many as he had fingers on his right hand. Then more appeared, and he saw as many as his fingers on both hands.

They were coming straight toward him. He stood as though
frozen in his tracks. The biggest animal, the one in the lead,
stopped and sniffed the air suspiciously.

Akavak turned. He crouched and moved quickly out of their

line of sight. Then he stumbled hurriedly along the gully to the little snowhouse.

"Grandfather! Grandfather!" Akavak called as he crawled into the snowhouse. "There are musk ox. Many of them. Just beyond the gully."

"I cannot stand up this morning, boy," his grandfather said in a quivering voice. "Perhaps it is because I am cramped from not moving, and the lamp is out of oil and it is cold in here. I fell down when I tried to leave the house, and now I cannot rise."

Akavak knelt beside his grandfather and placed his hand on his cheek. It felt cold, and his eyes seemed weak and dim.

"What shall I do, Grandfather? What shall I do?" Akavak said again. "All that meat stands there before us. Can I kill them with the seal harpoon?"

For a long time there was no answer. Then his grandfather said softly, "Never. Their weight would break it like a sliver of thin ice. Bring the rolled skin into the house. Bring me my staff."

Akavak hurried out and returned with the staff.

"Try to bend it," said the old man.

Akavak tried, but it was now frozen solid.

"I cannot bend it," said Akavak. "It is hard as whalebone."

"Good. Now take the sealskin lacings from my boot tops and tie them together. Has the wind blown the tundra moss free of snow?" he asked.

"Yes," said Akavak.

"Good," said his grandfather again. "Then the musk ox have come up to feed on the high plateau after the storm. They should stay near us for a while."

The old man drew the sharp stone blade from beneath the sleeping skin and tried to bind it to the frozen staff, but he was too weak, and his hands trembled.

"Here, boy, you lash this blade. Do it strongly, mind you, for it could mean your life to have it slip."

When Akavak had bound the rough spearhead into place, his grandfather said, "Now take the water from beneath the ice in the horn cup and pour it over the lashings. Quickly stand the spear outside, and the bindings will swell and freeze."

Having placed the spear outside, Akavak crawled inside the house again, and his grandfather said to him, "Musk ox are strange, lonely beasts who live far from men. Our people do not know well how to hunt them, for we rarely see them. It is wrong that a boy such as you should have to go alone after them while his grandfather rests like a child in the snowhouse. But there is no help for it. Today I could not even crawl to them, and the musk ox are our only chance to live.

"I cannot tell you what these strong animals will do when you go close to them. Sometimes they will attack you, sometimes they will run away from you, and sometimes they will stand on the open plain and form a circle to protect their young. I have never seen them make such a circle, but hunters say it is the worst and most dangerous time of all.

"Do not throw that spear. Keep it, for you may need it a second time. If a musk ox attacks you, kneel and place the butt of the spear firmly on the ground and allow the animal to run onto the point. Here, take my short knife and my hunting bag. Go with strength," he whispered, and he lay down once more in the cold.

Akavak left the snowhouse, quickly replacing the snow door. As he walked up the gully, he said to himself, "I will not return to that igloo until I have food. Only with food will I return."

The fog swirled thickly across the plateau, and Akavak, light-headed with hunger, started to run. He feared that he had lost the herd.

Suddenly the musk ox appeared again through the fog. He was almost beside them, and they snorted in fear and anger at being disturbed by this strange creature. The big bull that led them stood watching beneath the immense curve of its humped shoulders. Its long dark-brown hair trailed almost to the snow, nearly covering short, powerful legs. Its huge horns were joined together by a massive plate of bone that protected the front of its skull from where they swept downward, then curved upward into two sharp points.

Akavak was so close that he could see the bull's nostrils widen as it blew out clouds of breath into the freezing air. Its eyes rolled wildly, showing the whites, as its hoofs angrily flung up clots of snow.

A calf bawled out in alarm. The big bull ran in a short circle herding the young males, females, and their offspring into a tight group. Shoulder to shoulder they stood, with the calves protected in the middle. Any outside enemy would have to meet their deadly horns.

Akavak knelt down in front of the musk ox. He dug his spear into the frozen ground and waited. Nothing happened. He called out to them, but still nothing happened. He dared not throw his spear at them, and yet they would not attack him.

Some of the musk ox lost interest because Akavak did not smell or act like their only known enemy, the wolf. They began to eat the rough tundra moss and then broke their circle and started to move down the high plateau. But they were nervous and watchful and kept a good distance between themselves and this stranger.

Akavak trailed after the herd, not knowing how to approach them again. He could see through a clearing in the fog that they would soon cross a part of the glacier, and he feared that he would lose them.

With a desperate shout, he ran straight toward them. The musk ox milled around, and the big bull, with its instinct for protection, once again forced the others into a close circle. They stood heads down, carefully eying Akavak.

Then suddenly they stiffened and shifted their weight, spreading their feet wide, ready for an attack. They snorted nervously, but they did not seem to be watching Akavak any more. Quickly he looked around. He saw a gray form crouched in the snow less than a sled's length from him. Its hair bristled. The end of its tail flipped nervously back and forth. Its yellow eyes seemed to glow with madness.

Akavak stared in wonder and in fright, for it was the dog Kojo, half crazy with hunger, come to join in the kill. The dog crept forward on its belly like a wolf. Then, with its ears back and a low growl in its throat, it rushed straight at the big bull. It swerved just in time to escape the terrible twisting thrust of the sharp horns. The dog ran in a circle and just as swiftly attacked again. This time the big bull was ready for him. It rushed out of the circle straight at the dog that raced past Akavak. Kojo was caught between the terrible horns. Before Akavak's eyes, the great beast flung up his head, tossing Kojo in the air like a child's toy.

The head of the musk ox was still up, exposing its throat, as it rushed at Akavak. Dropping quickly onto one knee, he drove the butt of the spear against the frozen tundra and held fast. He felt the spear shaft buckle in his hands, but not before it had driven the sharply pointed stone blade deep into the animal's throat.

Akavak rolled aside to avoid the sharp flaying hoofs. He watched helplessly as the animal turned to renew its attack, for the bent spear shaft that lay beside him was without its point. Then he saw the musk ox stagger, and dark artery blood gushed

out over the snow. The great bull stumbled to its knees. With a mighty sigh, its spirit rushed out of its body, and it was dead.

The other musk ox had broken their circle, and Akavak saw the last of them disappearing into the swirling mists.

He stood up and walked slowly toward the great black beast that lay on the snow before him. At that moment, he also saw the dog Kojo limping toward the kill. The two creatures, man and dog, eyed each other. Kojo reached the fallen animal first and stood there snarling. Akavak raised his hand and called a command to the dog, but it would not obey him.

Weak and starving, Akavak watched the dog slowly eat his fill of the meat. When Kojo had finished, he stared at Akavak as if in triumph. Then with a low growl, he turned and stalked slowly off into the mist.

Akavak shook with excitement as he knelt, quickly cut away, and devoured strips of the warm meat. With his knife, he removed the stone spearhead from the big animal's throat. Then he cut out the liver and removed a heavy layer of rich back fat that he knew would make fuel for the lamp. He severed the spine with the stone blade and cut away the animal's hindquarters. These he tied by the feet to the end of the spear.

Although the load weighed as much as he did, the warm meat had given him strength and hope, and he was eager to get the food back to his grandfather. He found that the meat slipped easily over the hard-packed drifts. The sun was high, showing pale yellow through the mists above him, when he reached the igloo.

"Grandfather! Grandfather! I have meat for you," Akavak

called as he cut open the door and crawled inside the snowhouse, dragging the huge hindquarters of the musk ox after him.

The igloo was freezing cold, though it glowed inside with the pale light of the afternoon sun. The old man stared at Akavak from his caribou-skin wrapping. But he was pale, his lips were blue, and he did not speak or seem to recognize him. Akavak gently fed him some soft strips of liver. He then whirled the bow drill until it made smoke and a small flame, and he lighted the old wick and fed it with the back fat from the musk ox. Slowly the fat melted and flowed until the lamp burned brightly, filling the small igloo with warmth and light. Holding the horn cups over the heat, Akavak made a rich blood soup and fed this slowly to his grandfather.

He could see and feel the warmth return to his grandfather's cheeks and hands. Soon the old man smiled, and finally he was able to sit up, and all of his senses returned to him.

Akavak ate more of the delicious meat and trimmed the wick in the lamp so that it would burn throughout the night.

He lay down beside his grandfather. Before he went to sleep, he thought for a long time of his sister, and so vivid were his thoughts that she seemed to appear before him, standing small and alone on the snow, as he had seen her last on the day of his leaving.

In the morning, his grandfather was hungry again. He drank the thick soup they made and ate more meat with Akavak.

When Akavak went out of the snowhouse, he saw the dog lying in the snow. Kojo stood up, stretched, wriggled his body, and licked his lips in a friendly way.

"Grandfather, the dog is back," called Akavak.

"Good. Feed him some meat," answered his grandfather.

Akavak cut a portion from the lower leg and threw it to Kojo, who wolfed it down, curled up on the snow, and went to sleep.

Akavak looked up at the sky with a great feeling of relief, for now he believed that they had both escaped from the evil powers of the mountains.

That night in the snowhouse when they ate again, Akavak told his grandfather every detail of the musk-ox hunt and how the dog had helped him.

The old man listened carefully to each word and was silent for a long time. Then, slowly beating time with his hands, he sang an ancient song that he had once heard from the far northern people, the ones who live behind the sun:

> "Ayii, Ayii, Ayii,
> I wish to see the musk ox run again.
> It is not enough for me
> To sing of the dear beasts.
> Sitting here in the igloo
> My songs fade away,
> My words melt away,
> Like hills in fog.
> Ayii, Ayii, Ayii."

"That song is old, and yet its words suit me very well," said the grandfather.

They drifted off to sleep, and Akavak dreamed of the terrible blue abyss. In his dream, he looked over the edge and imagined he saw the sled floating, suspended forever in blue shadows.

When he awoke, he took Kojo's long dog line, and the harpoon with its line, and headed toward the glacier. The dog followed him. It took him a little time to find the hole again, for their tracks had been filled in by the storm. When he saw it, he was almost afraid to go near, so vivid and terrible were his memories of that place. He felt his way forward with the harpoon. Then he lay down and crawled to the edge, where he could look into the gaping hole.

There hung the sled, almost as he had seen it in his dream. It was wedged tightly between the icy walls of the giant crack. He thought with sadness of the dogs that must be lying far below under the pile of fallen snow. He studied the position and angle of the sled for some time, noticing that one runner did not touch the ice wall.

Carefully he tied a strong slip knot in the sealskin harpoon line, and this he tied to the end of the long dog line. Holding his breath, he lowered the knotted line and slipped it over the end of the wooden sled runner. Cautiously he drew the line upward until he saw the noose tighten. Then he attached the dog line to Kojo's harness, and together they pulled the sled free and hauled it slowly out of the crack.

Akavak pushed the sled away from the dangerous hole and danced with delight when he saw that the other dog lines were still attached to it. Also the big white bearskin, the lamp, the extra sleeping skins, and the mitts his sister had given him were still lashed in place.

"With this sled, I shall leave these mountains," he said to himself again and again. "I shall take my grandfather out of these mountains, and we shall go to his brother's land."

When his grandfather looked out of the igloo and saw the sled, he sat up and said in a trembling voice, "I had given up hope of seeing my brother, but look, the mountain spirits may wish to give us back our lives again." And he clapped his hands with joy.

65

That night his grandfather crawled out of the snowhouse and stood up, supporting himself with the harpoon shaft as he leaned against Akavak. The sky was clear and full of stars. The old man looked up and pointed at the bright north star, then lowered his arm straight down until his shaking finger pointed to a narrow pass between two hills.

"There, through that pass we shall travel north again across the plateau. Below that star lies the giant river Kokjuak that flows past my brother's camp."

Akavak fed the dog well and crawled into the snowhouse. In preparation for the journey, he began cutting wide strips from the bearskin with which to fashion a harness for himself. He sharpened a needle from a splinter of musk-ox bone and drew fine strong sinew from the musk-ox leg. With these he sewed the harness together. His sewing was crude, for all sewing in their camp was done by the women, and he wished that his mother could be there to help him.

In the morning, he harnessed the dog, loaded the lamp and the precious meat, and with the bearskin made a comfortable place for his grandfather to lie on the sled. When this was done, he helped the old man out of the snowhouse and urged him to lie down on the sled, while he carefully covered him with skins.

All that day Akavak and the dog struggled across the high plateau, and so hard did they work that they did not feel the biting cold. When the sun set and the mountains cast blue shadows across the snow, they stopped to build a snowhouse. But the old man was so paralyzed by the cold that he could not help. Akavak worked alone until the igloo was completed. It took him

a long time to light the lamp and to feed his grandfather, for now he had to do everything by himself.

"Tomorrow, if the wind does not rise, we will reach the far edge of the mountain. Tomorrow. Tomorrow," the old man mumbled again and again.

On the following day, it was much warmer, without a breath of wind, and Akavak's grandfather seemed stronger. He sat up on the sled and even tried to push with his hands to ease the load when they crossed a difficult drift.

All day Akavak pulled beside the sled dog, Kojo. Akavak's harness cut into his shoulders painfully, and he thought at times

that he could walk no more. But in his mind he kept thinking, "We are closer now. This journey nears its end."

Slowly they made their way forward through the twilight until they rounded a small hill. There lay the sight they had so long awaited. It was the end of the plateau. Akavak's grandfather let out a broken cry of triumph. The mountains were behind them, and the snow-covered plateau ended sharply against a line of sky.

"That is the edge. I remember the edge," he cried.

Even the tired dog seemed to understand and strained against the harness until darkness, when they reached the very edge of the plateau where the mountain slopes ran down toward the sea.

The small igloo Akavak built that night was quick and crude, for he planned to leave it as soon as there was light. They fed the dog and ate the musk-ox flesh again and slept. Akavak awoke once in the night, hearing his grandfather call out his brother's name as he moaned and turned in the darkness.

Dawn came slowly into the eastern sky, lighting the cracks in the dome of the snowhouse. Akavak cut away the door and crawled out. In all his life, he had never seen such a sight. The immense sky stretched around him like an endless blue bowl spanning the land and the frozen sea. As he watched, the coast far below turned pink and gold in the first rays of the morning sun.

"Look! Look! The river. The Kokjuak," cried the old man who had crawled out beside his grandson.

"And there are the snowhouses," said Akavak, pointing to a place near the sea. "Up here the land is still held in the grip of winter, but down below on the coast, there are signs of spring."

"Now," said his grandfather. "Now comes the hardest part of all, for the snow on the mountainside is deep and treacherous, with countless rocks hidden from our view. If the sled goes too fast and you lose control, all will be lost.

"Cut half of the bearskin into wide strips and twist them together into a great rope to hold loose in front of the runners. That will help to slow us down. Break the harpoon shaft and lash both halves together across the front of the sled so you can have a pair of handles to hold onto and guide us. Tie the dog on a short line, and be sure his harness is tight. He will be afraid and will help us to hold back the sled.

"I am ashamed that I cannot help you. You must lash me

70

tightly to the sled, for if I fall off, you will not be able to stop and return for me."

Akavak made the preparations. He noticed when he started to draw the long lashings tight that his grandfather turned away his face and quickly drew his right hand free, for he hated to be completely bound and helpless in the face of such danger.

A moment later he turned to Akavak once more and said softly, "I believe now that I may reach my brother's camp. For me it is like returning home again, as I shall see my younger brother in the land of our youth. Just now, like a dream before my eyes, I seemed to see again the two of us running across the soft tundra during the midsummer moon. We were chasing the big molting ganders with their black necks outstretched. I fell first into a shallow pond, and my brother laughed so hard that he fell in beside me. That is how life was with us when we were growing up. We were never apart.

"But best of all," said his grandfather, "I believe now that you will live to walk beyond these mountains, that you will return to our family, and that your children will carry within them the spirits of their ancestors."

"*Ukshavok.* It should be so," answered Akavak.

Holding the harpoon handles, Akavak cautiously eased the heavily loaded sled over the edge of the steep downward slope. He lay out almost flat on his back, digging his heels into the snow before him. The dog howled in terror and drew back behind the sled, digging his paws into the snow, fighting to break their downward speed.

Akavak flung the twisted bearskin rope under the runners.

When the strain was so great that Akavak thought he must let go or have his arms dragged from their sockets, they struck a big stone, swerved, and halted. He had to fling his weight against the sled to prevent it from rolling over. Here they rested among the sharp black rocks, exposed by the recent windstorm. He looked at his grandfather, lashed to the sled, almost hidden in the fur robes, and the old man smiled weakly and nodded to him.

Fearfully Akavak started the sled on the last terrible run down the mountain. He cut across the slope, and then, with a tremendous effort, he turned the sled and went in the other direction, leaving a large zigzag trail on the mountainside. Again he used the twisted bearskin beneath the runners to break their speed.

Then suddenly the slowing rope slipped from his grasp. Akavak lost control, and the heavy sled rushed down the mountain, dragging Akavak and Kojo with it. It thundered over glare ice, flew silently over deep snow, and did not stop until it hit some bare rocks. There it almost overturned, but its speed was halted, and Akavak gained control once more.

He was wet with sweat. Snow was packed in his sleeves and filled the neck of his parka. But as he wiped his face clean and looked back at his long curving track down the mountain, he saw that the worst was past. Before him lay the flat coast and the giant river that flowed into the sea. They were saved.

Akavak drove his weight against the sled once more and knelt on the side, pushing with one foot. The sled moved so fast that it passed the dog who raced forward trying to keep out of the way of the bounding runners.

Akavak could see the people of the tiny village hurrying out of their houses and running toward him in great excitement, for they had never seen a loaded sled pulled by one dog arrive from the mountains.

Their momentum carried the sled right into the middle of the camp, where the people clustered. The strange dogs circled and sniffed and snarled at Kojo, but he stood aloof among them like a lean gray wolf.

An old man came forward, his arms upraised in greeting. He called out, "Relative! Nephew of mine. You have arrived."

Akavak got off the sled and said to him, "We have arrived, great uncle of mine. At last I see you."

They stood before each other, and Akavak saw that this man was almost the image of his grandfather.

Whirling, he started to undo the lines he had so carefully tied to hold his grandfather on the sled. The others gathered around him. Quickly Akavak turned back the caribou skin that half covered the old man's face. His grandfather's eyes were still open, but now they stared blankly at the sky, seeing nothing. Akavak felt his cheek. It was freezing cold. He grasped his grandfather's hand, but that, too, was icy cold. The white clutched fingers seemed to reach out as if in readiness to greet his brother.

Akavak's whole body began to tremble and shake as though he stood naked in a freezing wind. His throat was so tight that he could not speak. Silently he pointed at the stiffened hand.

His great uncle bent down and gently covered his brother's face with the caribou skin. The women in the camp huddled together, and from them rose a great wailing as they drew their hoods over their faces. Then there was silence.

The brother pulled away the last lashing that held Akavak's grandfather to the sled. He raised his arms slowly and sang out in a strong voice:

"Ayii, Ayii,
Arise, Arise,
With movements
Swift as a raven's wing,
Arise to meet the day.
Turn your face
From the dark of night
To gaze at the dawn
As it whitens the sky.
Arise, Arise,
Ayii, Ayii."

Akavak looked once more at the form of his grandfather, lying lifeless on the sled, then turned away with a terrible feeling of loneliness.

The old women and some young girls led him up to the big sealskin tent that stood on a dry gravel bank, near the winter snowhouses that now were crumbling in the warmth of the spring sun. A small flock of snowbirds migrating from the south landed near the tent. Torrents of water from the melting snow cut curving paths toward the sea. Everywhere around him were the soft signs of spring, as the new season advanced across the land. To Akavak it seemed as though the whole world was being born again.

Before he entered the tent, he turned and looked up at the mountains. They stood like ancient giants guarding some forbidden place. White clouds soared across their peaks. The mountains were different for him now. He had climbed them and lived within them. He had almost died there. From those great heights, he had looked down at the world like a wind spirit and had seen all of the land and the vast distances of the frozen sea. After that he had come down from the mountains. But now, like his grandfather, he had a strong secret feeling for the white plateau. And he knew that his vision of the great black beasts running on the high plain would stay with him forever.

He entered and sat down wearily on the soft skins that covered the wide bed, and the young women removed his damp boots and stood shyly near him. In the warmth of the tent, he drank the hot brown soup they offered him and ate the delicate meat of a young seal.

He stared into the flame of the big stone lamp, watching it shimmer and dance like waves on the sea in summer. No longer did he tremble from cold and fear and hunger. He lay back on the warm caribou skins, and as he fell asleep, he dreamed that he took his grandfather's hand and together they soared upward— upward and across the ancient mountains, over the whiteness of the glacier, and out among the stars.

canadian/ indian and eskimo arts and crafts

the snow goose

40 elgin street, ottawa 4 - 232-2213